P9-CAM-797

my LITTLE PONY

FRIENDSHIP is MAGIC

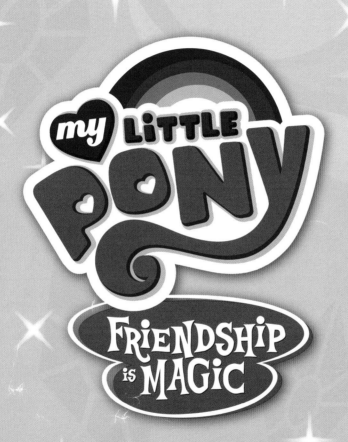

ABDOPUBLISHING.COM

Reinforced library bound edition published in 2018 by Spotlight, a division of ABDO, PO Box 398166, Minneapolis, Minnesota 55439. Spotlight produces high-quality reinforced library bound editions for schools and libraries. Published by agreement with Little, Brown and Company.

Printed in the United States of America, North Mankato, Minnesota.
092017   012018

THIS BOOK CONTAINS
RECYCLED MATERIALS

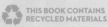

Licensed By:

LITTLE, BROWN & COMPANY

LB kids™
NEW YORK BOSTON
lb-kids.com

Little, Brown and Company

Hachette Book Group, 1290 Avenue of the Americas, New York, NY 10104. LB kids is an imprint of Little, Brown and Company. The LB kids name and logo are trademarks of Hachette Book Group, Inc.

PUBLISHER'S CATALOGING IN PUBLICATION DATA

Names: Belle, Magnolia, author. | Rogers, Amy Keating, author. | Hasbro Studios, illustrator.
Title: Crusaders of the lost mark / writer, Magnolia Belle ; writer, Amy Keating Rogers ; art, Hasbro Studios.
Description: Reinforced library edition. | Minneapolis, Minnesota : Spotlight, 2018. | Series: My little pony picture books
Summary: Join Scootaloo, Sweetie Belle, and Apple Bloom as the Cutie Mark Crusaders continue their quest to discover their special talent.
Identifiers: LCCN 2017943449 | ISBN 9781532141003
Subjects: LCSH: Picture book--Juvenile fiction. | Ponies--Juvenile fiction. | Abilities--Juvenile fiction.
Classification: DDC [E]--dc23
LC record available at https://lccn.loc.gov/2017943449

Spotlight
A Division of ABDO
abdopublishing.com

CRUSADERS OF THE LOST MARK

Based on the episode "Crusaders of the Lost Mark"
by **Amy Keating Rogers**
Adapted by **Magnolia Belle**

LITTLE, BROWN & COMPANY
LB kids

ABDO
Spotlight

Apple Bloom, Scootaloo, and Sweetie Belle are in their clubhouse reviewing what they've done to find their cutie marks.

"We've tried to do most everything, but if we keep tryin', we'll find our marks, Cutie Mark Crusaders!" Apple Bloom reassures them.

Pipsqueak runs into the clubhouse and shouts, "Cutie Mark Crusaders! I need your help! I'm running for student pony president against Diamond Tiara! Would you be my campaign managers?"

"We never tried getting our cutie marks in campaign managin' before. Let's do it, Crusaders!" Apple Bloom announces.

Soon after, students are gathered in the school yard listening to Pipsqueak speak.

"If I'm elected student pony president, I'll go to the school board and get our playground equipment all fixed up!"

"Oh yeah? Well, if Diamond Tiara is voted in, we will put a statue of her in the center of the school yard!" Silver Spoon says, scoffing at the other ponies.

Diamond Tiara pulls Silver Spoon aside and scolds her. "Silver Spoon! That was my big announcement for when I won!"

"Gosh, I'm sorry. I was only trying to help," Silver Spoon says sheepishly.

Diamond Tiara is annoyed. "Well, I don't need that kind of help!"

"Do we really want a big statue of Diamond Tiara, or would we rather have new playground equipment?" Scootaloo asks the other students.

Sweetie Belle rallies the ponies. "A vote for Pip is a vote for the playground!"

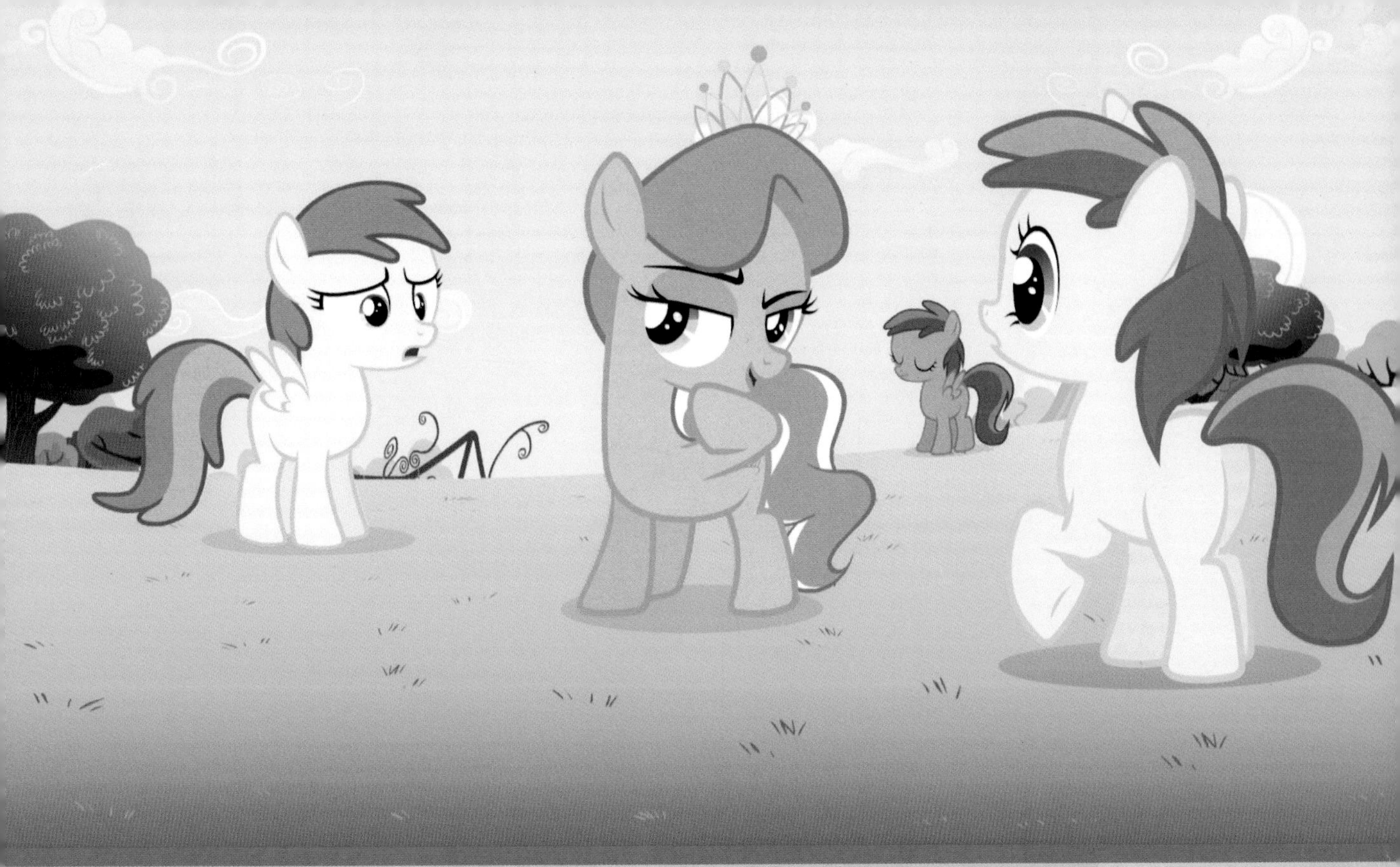

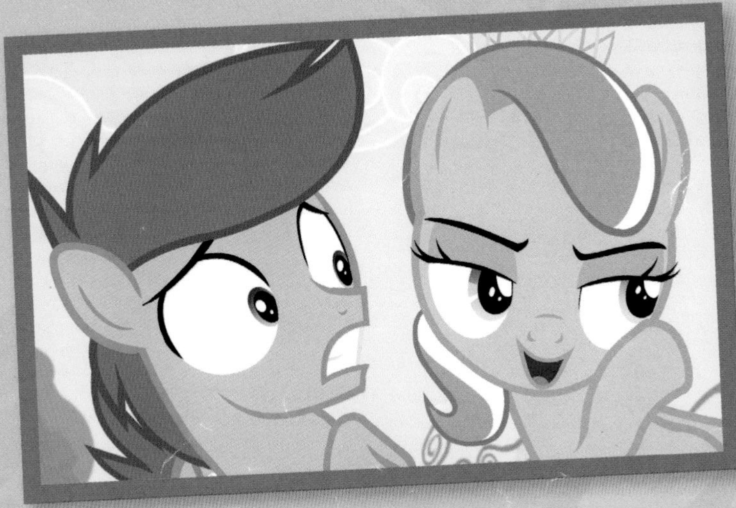

Since Diamond Tiara knows that the Cutie Mark Crusaders are swaying the voters, she tries to intimidate her fellow students.

"Vote for me," she cries, "unless you want all your secrets revealed!"

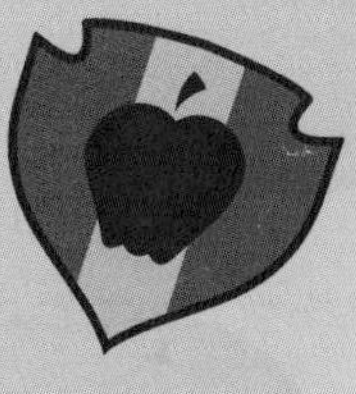

Silver Spoon tries to help Diamond Tiara again. "You can win the whole election if you just show the students that you really care..."

"I don't recall asking you to speak!" Diamond Tiara snaps at Silver Spoon, then storms away to vote.

The Cutie Mark Crusaders see that Silver Spoon's feelings are hurt.

"When you're votin'," Apple Bloom says to her, "please consider voting for kindness and a pony who will listen."

Miss Cheerilee comes out of the schoolhouse. "The votes have been counted, and the results are in! The new student pony president is"—she pauses for suspense—"Pipsqueak!"

The students all cheer. "Hip, hip, hooray for President Pip!"

The Cutie Mark Crusaders look at their flanks, but they're still blank. They're disappointed they didn't get campaign manager cutie marks.

Diamond Tiara can't believe she lost the election. She asks Miss Cheerilee for a revote, since it's obvious to her the results are wrong.

The teacher feels bad for her student but tells her that Pipsqueak won fair and square.

Scootaloo is concerned about Diamond Tiara. "We should make sure she's okay."

"Yeah, just 'cause she's never cared about anypony else's feelings doesn't mean we shouldn't care about hers," Apple Bloom adds.

Diamond Tiara's mother, Spoiled Rich, is very upset about her daughter's defeat. "You mean I bought all these party supplies just to celebrate nothing?!"

Diamond Tiara sighs. "Sorry, Mother."

As she reflects on her actions, Diamond Tiara realizes her treatment of others impacted the vote. "I've made mistakes. I feel like a flawed diamond, but I just want to shine," she says.

"Poor thing. She wants to be better, but she doesn't know how," Apple Bloom laments over Diamond Tiara.

Sweetie Belle adds, "It seems like she could use a friend or two."

"Sounds like a job for the Cutie Mark Crusaders!" Scootaloo howls as all three raise their hooves.

Diamond Tiara accepts an invitation to the Cutie Mark Crusaders clubhouse. She is astonished as she looks at their cutie mark charts.

"You three are...really lucky," Diamond Tiara tells them.

The Cutie Mark Crusaders are surprised to hear this. "We are?" they ask in unison.

"Well, yeah, you get to learn who you really are before you're stuck with a cutie mark you don't understand." Diamond Tiara seems sad.

"Aw, Diamond, you just need to be true to your cutie mark. You have such strong powers of persuasion. You can do great things!" Apple Bloom says.

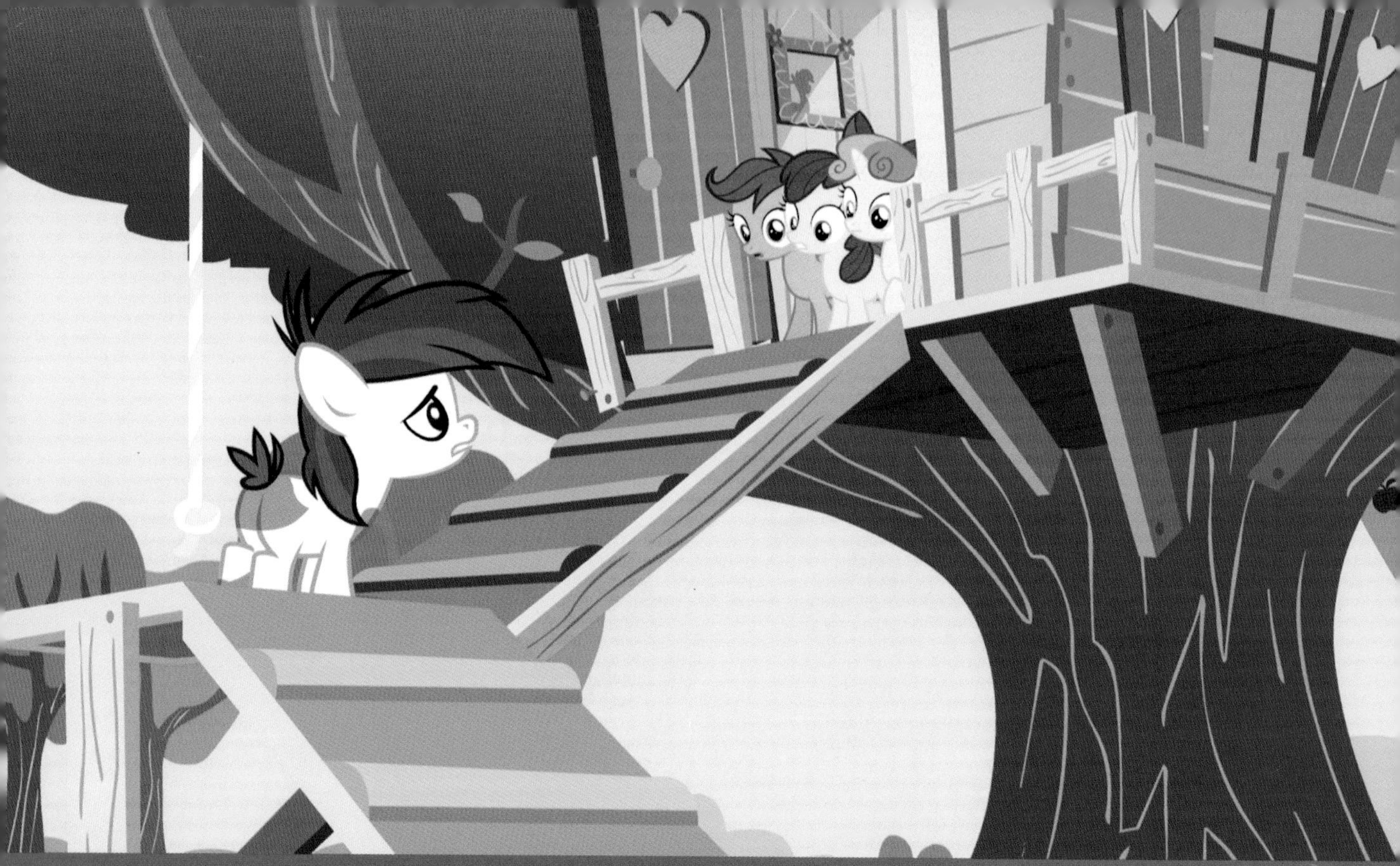

From outside the clubhouse, Pipsqueak shrieks, “Cutie Mark Crusaders! There’s no money in the school budget for new playground equipment! What do I do?”

“Don’t worry, Pip! It’ll be okay,” Sweetie Belle reassures him. “We’ll meet you back at school and help you find a solution!”

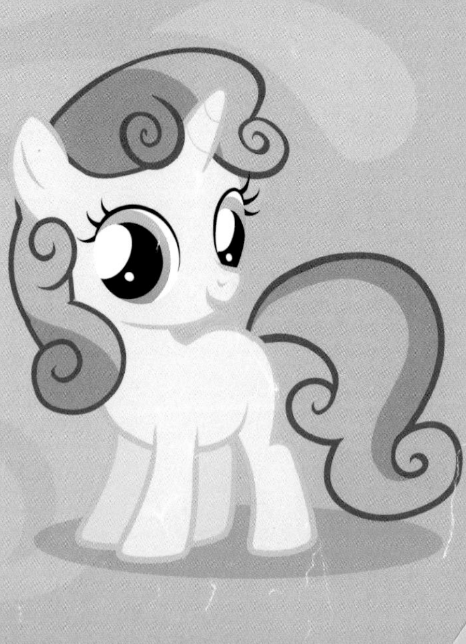

A grin flashes across Diamond Tiara's face. She bursts out of the clubhouse toward the school. The Cutie Mark Crusaders chase after her and remind her to be true to her cutie mark.

Diamond Tiara says, "You're working harder than anypony to get your cutie marks! I'm going to use my talent for persuasion to ask my father to donate money for the new playground!"

The Cutie Mark Crusaders watch proudly as brand-new playground equipment is delivered a few days later.

Apple Bloom wonders, "Maybe we should take some time off from worryin' about our cutie marks and help other ponies discover their true talents instead."

"Yeah, that's lots more fun and important than worrying about our own cutie marks!" Sweetie Belle exclaims.

Suddenly, a magic wind sweeps the Cutie Mark Crusaders up into the air. When it returns them to the ground, they discover that they now have... their cutie marks!

"Our cutie mark is the Cutie Mark Crusaders emblem!" they all shout.

When Rarity, Applejack, and Rainbow Dash see that the Cutie Mark Crusaders have their cutie marks, they are overcome with tears of joy. They throw a big party to celebrate, and everypony comes! Yay!

Sweetie Belle, Apple Bloom, and Scootaloo now know that their special talent is to help other ponies understand their cutie marks. Cutie Mark Crusaders forever!